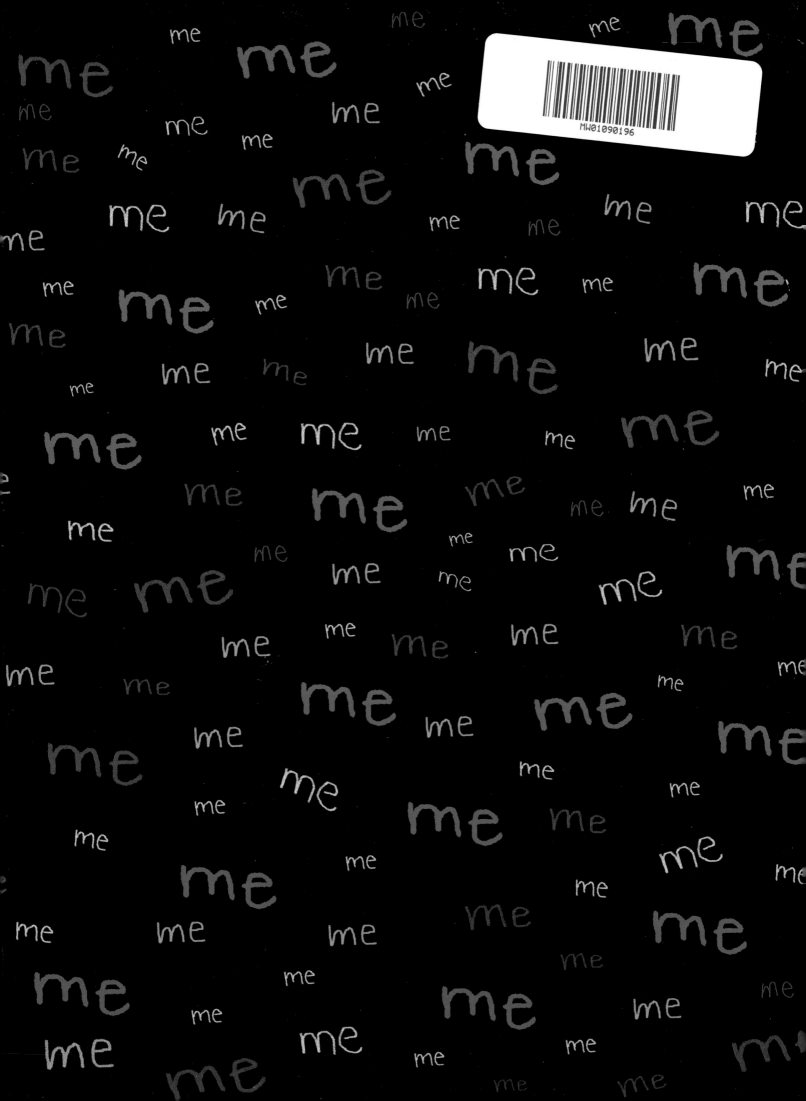

For Suvi Asch and Elliot Kreloff,
the design team who
collaborated on this book
—HMZ

Published in the United States 2006 by
Blue Apple Books
515 Valley Street, Maplewood, N.J. 07040
www.blueapplebooks.com
Distributed in the U.S. by Chronicle Books

Printed in China

ISBN 13: 978-1-59354-146-0
ISBN 10: 1-59354-146-5

3 5 7 9 10 8 6 4 2

HARRIET ZIEFERT

ME! ME! ABC

CHARACTERS BY
INGRI VON BERGEN

 BLUE APPLE BOOKS

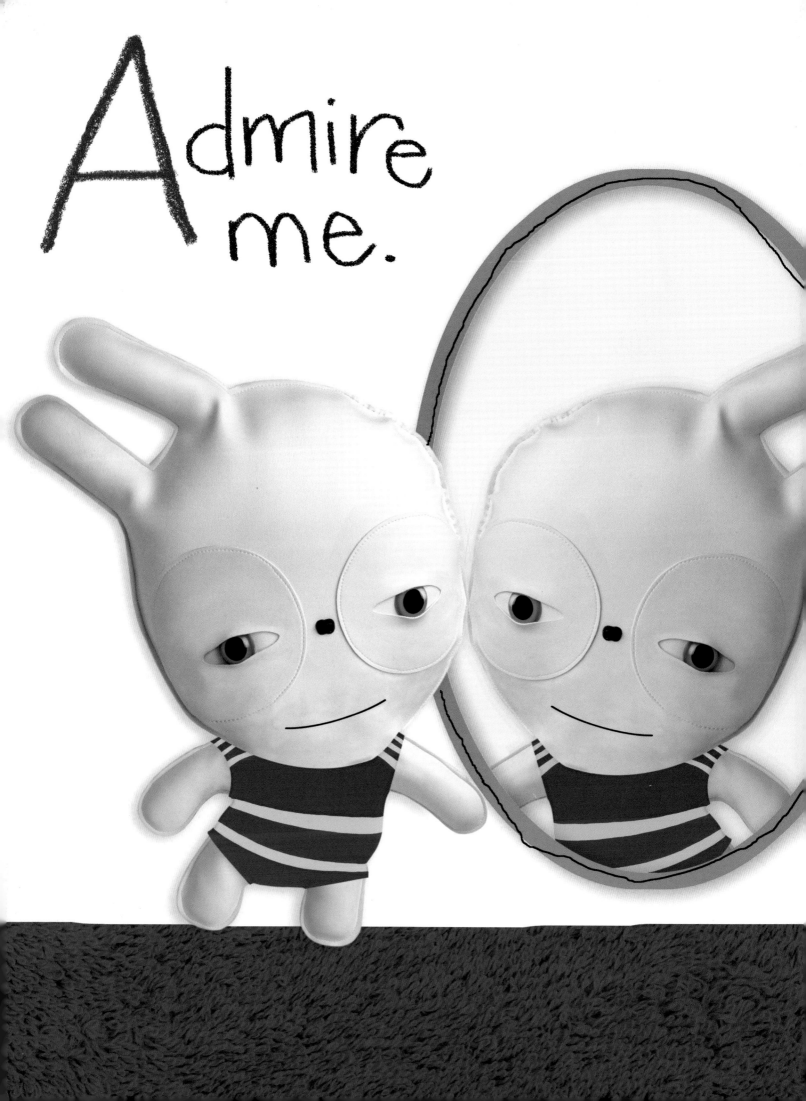

Buckle
me.

Call
me.

Dance
with me.

Follow me.

Hang
with
me.

Jump with me.

Miss
me.

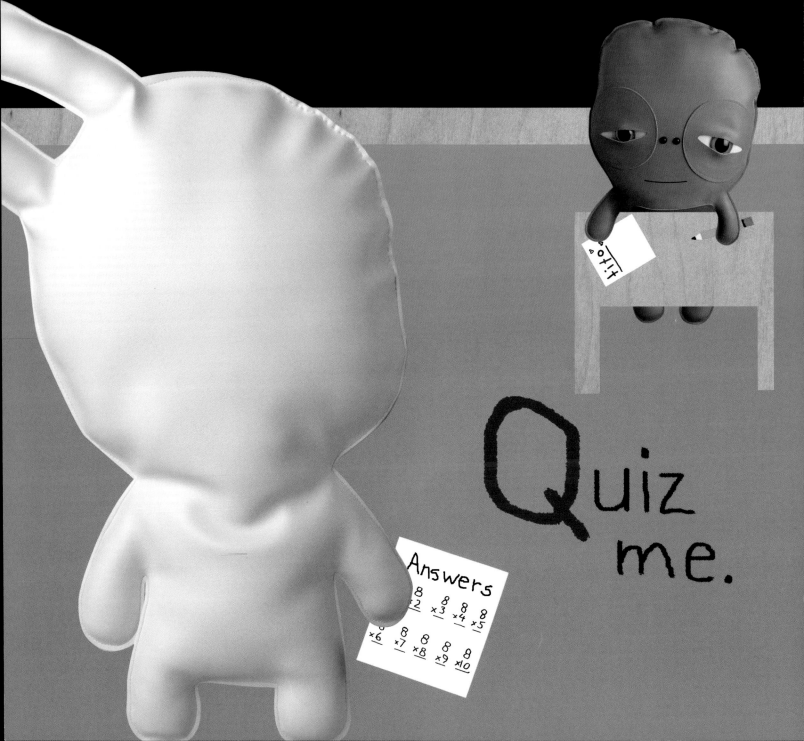

Skate with me.

eXercise with me.

Yippee for me!

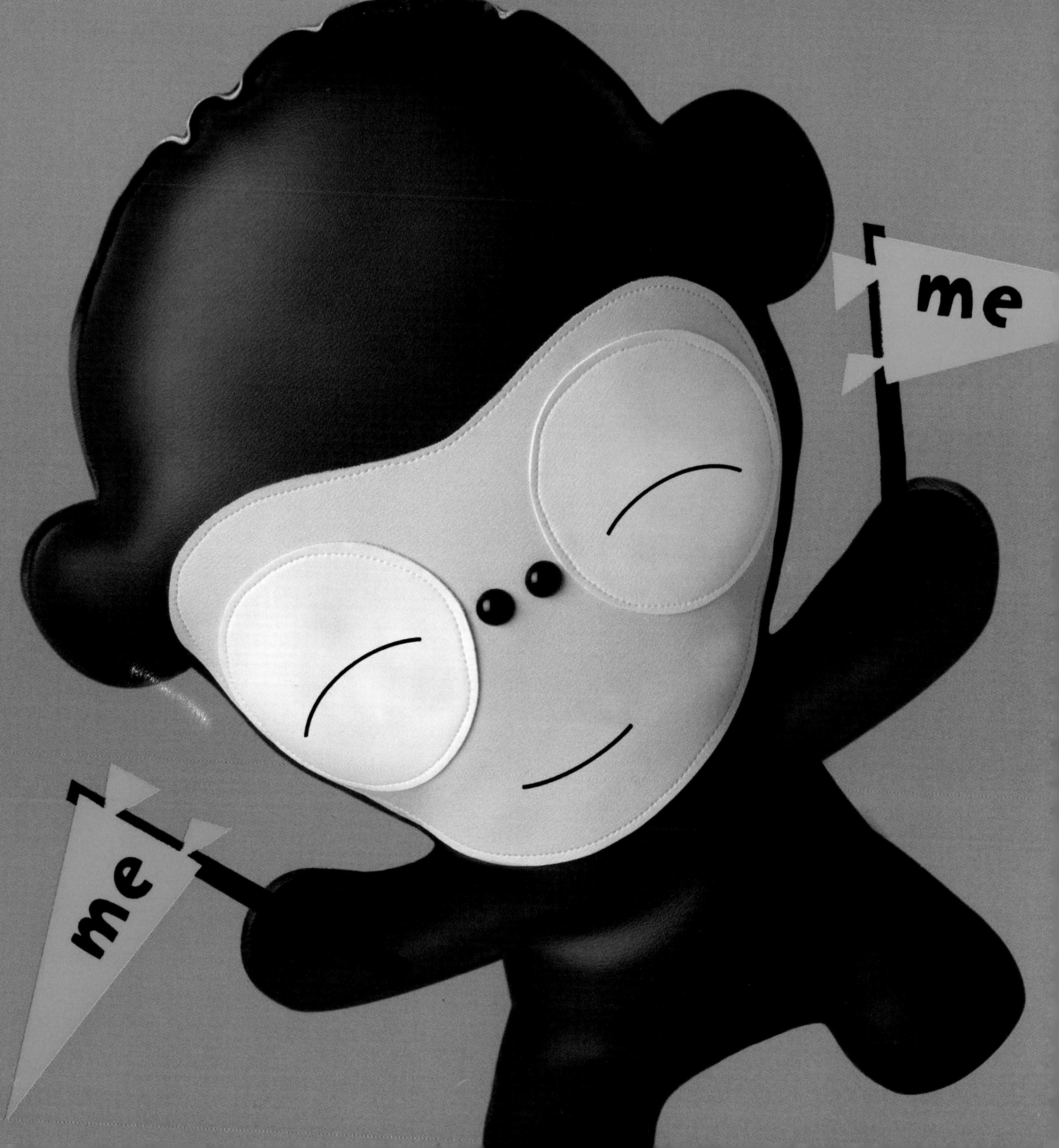

The End.

Marty

He isn't really naughty — just misunderstood.

Francis

Francis is a love bunny. Giving love is what Francis loves to do.

Moki + Miko

They like doing things together and are rarely found apart.

Tito Turtle

Tito Turtle is quite shy and prefers to stay in his shell. Once you get to know him, he's as friendly as can be.

Picco Panda

Picco Panda is good at almost everything, especially climbing trees and making kites.

Lilac

Lilac, the grumpy gorilla, can be difficult, but usually knows what's right.

Pig-Pig Piggy Pig

Pig-Pig Piggy Pig comes from a family of flying pigs, but she has no wings and can't fly with her family. So she hangs out with Francis, Picco Panda, and Tito Turtle.

Harriet Ziefert

bought several Ingri dolls when she was
visiting her new grandchild in Williamsburg, Brooklyn.
She discovered that Ingri lived there, too, and
then tracked her down on the Web.
Harriet likes to collaborate with artists in making books.
She has created an office environment that resembles
a Bauhaus atelier—a studio where artists, authors,
and designers come together to work. Ingri spent
several days in her office in Maplewood,
New Jersey, exchanging ideas with Harriet
and the design team there. As one of
them said, "*Me! Me! ABC* was a truly
collaborative effort." It speaks to
Harriet's conviction that the
best books are made when
author and artist can
speak freely and directly
to each other.

Ingri Von Bergen

was a doodler, photographer, and
animator before she became a toy maker.
She began making dolls as gifts for her
coworkers for the holidays. After great success at
a local craft fair, she decided to move to New York
and opened her own studio, House of Ingri.
About her creations, Ingri says, "It's a labor of love
to make these dolls; they don't come quick. I put a lot
of care in the details. They are each special to me
and I take the time on every one to make sure
they are the way they should be. There are
a lot of little things I do on each doll.
For instance, I make sure that
when I put Francis's eyes in,
his eyes line up with mine.
When I finish Lilac, I give
him a little hug and a pat
on the bum.
It makes a difference."

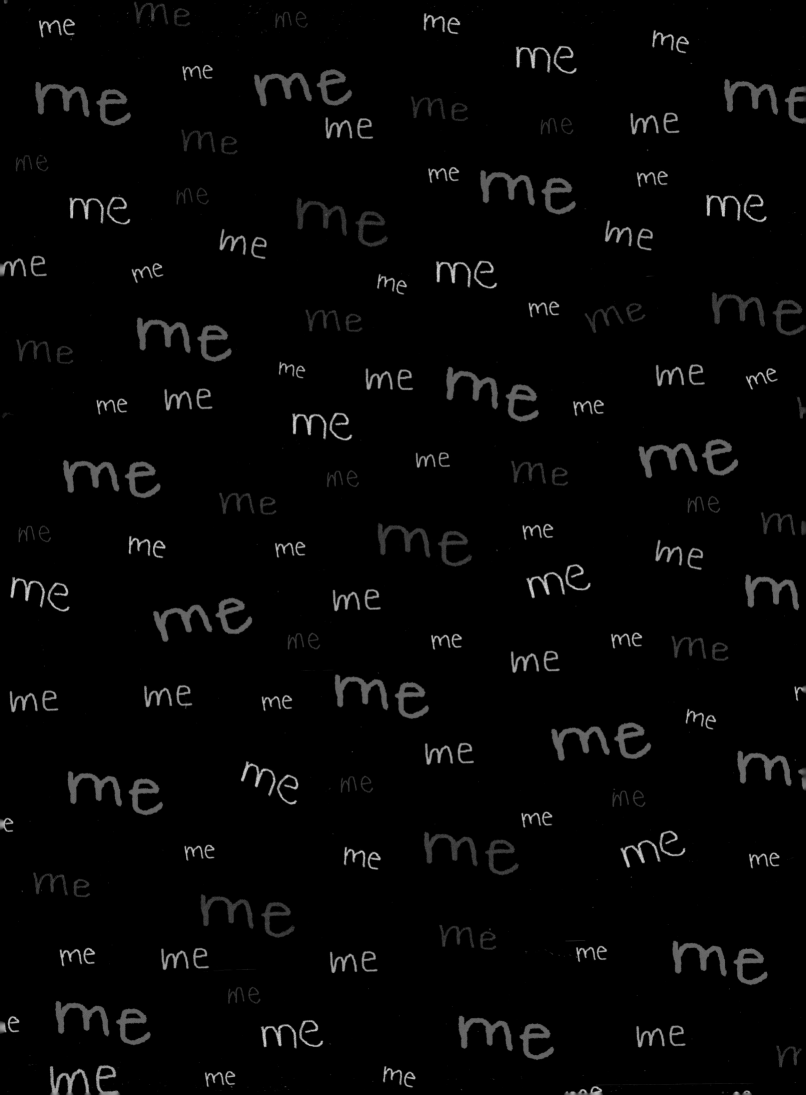